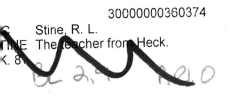

Look for these

ROTTEN SCHOOL

books, too!

ROTTEN SCHOOL

GROWTH LEARNING PIZZA!

THE TEACHER FROM HECK

R.L. STINE

Illustrations by Trip Park

HarperCollins*Publishers*
A Parachute Press Book

For Liz
–TP

The Teacher From Heck
Copyright © 2006 by Parachute Publishing, L.L.C.
Cover copyright © 2006 by Parachute Publishing, L.L.C.

For information address HarperCollins Children's Books, a division of HarperCollins
Publishers, 1350 Avenue of the Americas, New York, NY 10019.
www.harpercollinschildrens.com

Library of Congress Cataloging-in-Publication Data is available.
ISBN-10: 0-06-078821-6 (trade bdg.)—ISBN-10: 0-06-078822-4 (lib. bdg.)
ISBN-13: 978-0-06-078821-6 (trade bdg.)—ISBN-13: 978-0-06-078822-3 (lib. bdg.)

Cover and interior design by mjcdesign
1 2 3 4 5 6 7 8 9 10
❖
First Edition

— CONTENTS —

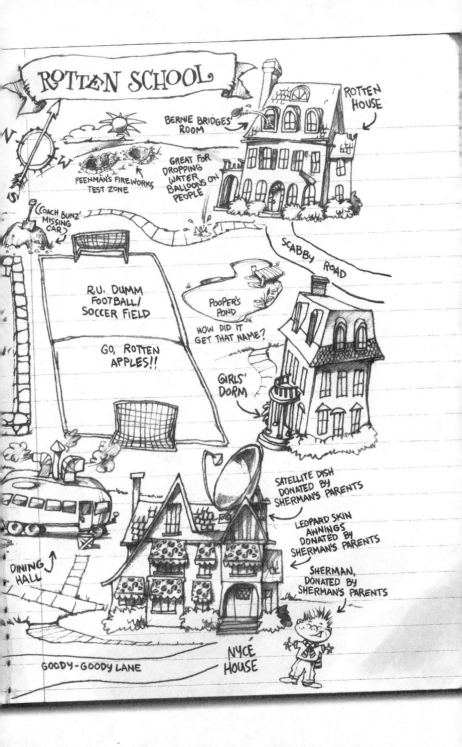

MORNING ANNOUNCEMENTS

Good morning, Rotten Students. This is Headmaster Upchuck. Please remember to make this day a Rotten day in every way. And now I'd like to get the day off to a Rotten start by reading the Morning Announcements....

Students who would like to join the After-School Big Butts Club can try out in the gym after classes today. You know what you have to bring.

1

Our wonderful cook, Chef Baloney, apologizes for sneezing into the pea soup yesterday. He says he's going to try really hard not to sneeze into the barley soup today.

Those students who sat in the audience and made frog-croaking noises during the choir concert yesterday—we know who you are, and we don't think it was funny.

Hammy the Hamster was successfully removed from second grader Chuck Stake's nose this morning. Chuck is feeling much better, and we're sure Hammy will be back to his old self in a week or two.

And finally, good news for all third graders. Our janitors tell me that the toilets in the third-grade bathrooms should be fixed in a week or two.

Chapter 1

MEET MR. SKRULOOSE

My name is Bernie Bridges, and you might wonder why I'm running so hard.

Normally I'd take time to enjoy the morning sunshine on the Great Lawn—to smell the sweet trees and flowers, to feel the warm breeze on my handsome face.

But this morning I am running full speed across the Rotten School campus.

I don't want to be late.

We have a new teacher. He is taking the place of our old teacher, Mrs. Heinie, and I want to be there early to welcome him. And to let him know that, yes, I'm a *leader* at this school. But I'm a leader who is willing to listen to my teacher once in a while.

In other words, I want to *suck up* to the new guy before Sherman Oaks and his pals get there.

You see, the Rotten School is a boarding school. We all live here on the campus.

I live with my friends in the coolest dorm— an old house called Rotten House. That rich, spoiled brat, Sherman Oaks, lives in the dorm called Nyce House.

Yuck. Who would want to live in a place called *Nyce* House? We hate every kid who lives there!

My feet pounded the grass. The School House rose up in front of me. That's what we call our classroom building.

4

A few seconds later, I slipped into my fourth-grade class.

Uh-oh. The room was full. Kids were already in their seats. They turned to watch me as I closed the door behind me.

I stared at the new teacher. Whoa! The dude was a *monster*! Give me a break! He was at least *eight feet tall* and built like a truck on top of a truck!

His Rotten School blazer stretched tightly across his massive chest. It looked ready to pop its buttons. I could see muscles rippling up and down his arms.

His name was written in chalk behind him.

MR. SKRULOOSE.

Skruloose?

I flashed him my best smile, the one with the adorable dimples. "Welcome, sir," I said. "I know I speak for everyone when I say how happy we are—"

"SHUT UP!"

he boomed, so loudly the windows rattled.

I swallowed my gum. He was kinda *rude*, don't you think?

His steel blue eyes narrowed in a hard stare. "You're in trouble," he growled.

I glanced all around. "Huh? Are you talking to me? I'm in trouble?"

What was his *problem*? What did I *do*?

Chapter 2

THE TEACHER FROM HECK

He glared at me. "You're ALMOST late to class."

"Almost?" I whimpered. "*Almost* late?"

Was this dude a little *weird*?

Mr. Skruloose pointed to the floor in front of me. "Soldier, drop down and give me ten," he ordered.

"Soldier? But my name is Bernie!"

He pointed to the floor. "Drop down and give me ten."

I blinked. "Ten *what*?"

"Soldier, give me ten push-ups."

"I was afraid of that," I said. I turned to my friend

Belzer at the next desk. "Belzer," I whispered, "drop down and give him ten push-ups for me."

"No problem," Belzer said.

Where would I be without good ol' Belzer?

The kid does *everything* for me. Brings me breakfast in bed…carries my backpack to class…It took *weeks* to put Belzer through his obedience-training. But it was worth it.

Belzer hit the floor and began straining to push his chunky body up. "One…uh…one and a half… one and three-quarters…"

"GET UP!" Mr. Skruloose boomed at Belzer. Two of his blazer buttons popped off and flew across the room. He gave me a cold stare. "In my class we do *our own* push-ups," he snarled.

I had no choice. I dropped to the floor. "It's kinda dusty down here, sir," I said. "Maybe I'd better not do this. Dust always makes me sneeze."

"SHUT UP!"

he roared again. "Give me ten!"

"Could we compromise on *three?*" I asked.

He didn't answer in words. Just growled.

I took that for a no. I dropped down and started giving him ten.

Skruloose marched back to his desk. Some kids saluted him, and he saluted back.

From down on the floor, I saw Sherman Oaks jump up from his seat in the front row. His parents pay extra so he can always sit in the front row. And they bought him a leopard-skin pillow to put on his chair so his butt doesn't get tired. I *told* you Sherman is a spoiled, rich brat.

Sherman walked up to Skruloose and pressed a few hundred-dollar bills into his hand. "Just a welcome present from me and my friends in Nyce House," Sherman said.

Sherman's blue eyes twinkled. He handed Mr. Skruloose a shiny, silver pen. "That's another gift for you. You can use it to write down my name. For when you make the Honor Roll list. It's Sherman Oaks."

Mr. Skruloose crinkled up the hundred-dollar bills

and shoved them into Sherman's mouth. "Are you trying to bribe me, soldier?" he boomed.

"MMMMPH-MMMMPH," Sherman replied.

"You might want to write down *my* name," Skruloose said. "My name is Mr. Skruloose. *No one* from my class ever makes the Honor Roll. I don't *believe* in giving good grades."

Sherman swallowed the hundred-dollar bills with a loud *gulp*. "You—you can't do this!" he sputtered. "I'm TOO RICH and too HANDSOME to be treated this way!"

I think that made Skruloose angry. His eyes bulged out of his head, he gritted his teeth, and his face turned the color of a tomato. He waved his meaty fists in the air.

Sherman took the hint. Shaking his head, he slunk back to his seat.

"NINE . . . TEN!" I shouted. I climbed into my seat. Actually, I only did two push-ups—but no one was looking.

Skruloose turned to the class. He loosened his school tie. Even his Adam's apple had muscles!

"Listen up, soldiers. I'm just a farm boy," he said.

"I come from Heck, Indiana. I guess you could call me The Teacher from Heck."

A few kids snickered at that. I groaned.

"But you'd better *not* call me that," Skruloose said. "I don't allow jokes in my classroom. And here are a few other things that I don't allow..."

He pulled out a long list and started to read:

"No glancing from side to side. No burping. No yawning. No blinking.

"No pencil-tapping on desks. No eraser-chewing.

"No sneezing. Always breathe through *both* nostrils.

"Never come *almost* late to class..."

I shook my head. I suddenly knew how to spell Skruloose...*N-U-T-S!*

No lie—he really *was* The Teacher from Heck!

How did this HAPPEN to us?

How did we lose Mrs. Heinie and get the toughest teacher in the world?

Well...it started a few days ago. It was all because of the Water War.

Chapter 3

WHAT IS A LETTUCE?

The Water War was on full blast. It was Rotten House against Nyce House in the wettest squirt-gun war in history. No one was safe. No one was *dry*!

We all walked around school totally soaked. Water dripped down our faces. Our wet sneakers squeaked on the floors.

Of course our teacher, Mrs. Heinie, didn't have a clue.

There are NO SQUIRT GUNS ALLOWED at the Rotten School.

So how did we have a squirt-gun war?

We had to be clever. And quick.

Every time Mrs. Heinie turned her back in class, someone got hit full blast in the face.

One day she was standing at the chalkboard making a list. "Now, who can tell me about the tomato?" she asked, squinting at us through her thick glasses. "Is the tomato a fruit or a vegetable?"

"It's a planet!" Wes Updood called out. "It revolves around the third moon of Vesuvio!"

Wes Updood is the coolest guy in school. But he's on a planet of his own. Maybe he comes from the Tomato Planet. No one can understand a word he says.

Mrs. Heinie shook her head. "Sorry, Wes, it's not a planet," she said. "Can anyone tell me about the tomato? Fruit or vegetable?"

Billy the Brain raised his hand. Billy knows everything.

"Actually," he said, "the tomato isn't a fruit *or* a vegetable. It's a kind of potato."

Mrs. Heinie let out a long sigh. She turned to the chalkboard and wrote *tomato* in the *Fruit* column.

As soon as she turned her back, we went to work.

I raised my watch, squeezed it, and squirted Sherman Oaks in the face with a spray of water. Wes Updood hiked up his belt buckle, squeezed it, and sprayed my pal Crench in the chest.

Crench pulled out his squirting MP3 player. He aimed a spray of water at Wes—missed—and hit the wall.

Kids laughed and cheered.

At the back of the room, I saw my friend Beast go to work. We call the guy Beast because we don't know if he's human or not. He's very furry for a human. And sometimes he bites if you make him angry.

Mrs. Heinie keeps him on a leash. But he's a good dude.

Beast picked up a bottle of water and squeezed the water into his mouth. Then he tilted his head up and spit a gusher of water over half the room.

Kids ducked and screamed.

Mrs. Heinie turned around and squinted through her thick glasses. "Is there a problem?" she asked.

"No. No problem," I said. I was mopping my desk with a towel.

"How about lettuce?" Mrs. Heinie asked. "Come on, class. Is lettuce a fruit or a vegetable?"

Billy the Brain raised his hand again. "Lettuce is actually an animal," he said. "That's because it has a head."

Sometimes I wonder about Billy the Brain. Maybe he needs a new nickname. Like Billy the Idiot.

Mrs. Heinie took off her glasses and rubbed her eyes. I pulled out my squirting pencil and gave Sherman a shot in the face.

Billy the Brain made all our secret squirting things. Thanks to him, just about *everything we own* squirts water!

Mrs. Heinie sighed and put her glasses back on. "People, the lettuce is *not* an animal," she said. "Does anyone—"

She stopped. She walked over to Billy the Brain, who sat at the end of the second row. She had her eyes on the laptop on Billy's desk.

Uh-oh.

Chapter 4

SWEETY WETS HIS PANTS

"You brought your laptop," Mrs. Heinie said. "Good. Let's look up *lettuce* and see what it says."

She reached for the laptop.

"No. Please—" Billy said. But he wasn't fast enough.

Mrs. Heinie leaned down. She started to type—and the laptop blasted her in the face with cold water!

Water splashed her glasses, ran down her cheeks, and drenched her sweater. She staggered back until she hit the wall. "What's going *on* here?" she shrieked.

Billy shrugged. "I've been having problems with my laptop," he said. "Why does it keep *doing* that?"

At lunch in the Dining Hall, Billy the Brain leaned over the table and whispered to me. "I have a new idea for a squirting weapon," he said. "Can you get me a lettuce?"

A squirting lettuce? Yeah, it sounds kinda dumb. But you can see the dude is always thinking, thinking, *thinking*!

Sherman and his Nyce House geeks were winning the Water War. My guys were dripping wet from morning to night. We needed to be clever. We needed some new ideas.

I took a bite of my salami sandwich. A shadow fell over the table. I looked up to see Joe Sweety hulking over me.

We call him The Big Sweety. But not to his face. Joe is the biggest,

meanest kid at Rotten School. He lives in Nyce House and is Sherman Oaks's good buddy.

Is Joe tough? Well, once I saw him punch out a tree because it wouldn't get out of his way.

"What's up, Sweety?" I said. "Had enough water battles? Did you come over to surrender?"

He didn't say anything. He just leaned over our table.

"HEY—!"

We all screamed as a powerful stream of water came shooting out of his nose. *Both nostrils!*

He soaked Feenman's pizza slice and my salami sandwich. Then he stood up, dried his nose with a tissue, and started to walk back to the Nyce House table.

"Hey, Sweety— that was *awesome!* How'd you do that?" Billy called.

Sweety turned around. He had a big grin on his meaty

face. "You losers should surrender," he said. "Sherman's parents bought us high-tech squirting weapons."

"What kind of weapons?" I asked.

"We've got *digital* squirters," Sweety bragged. "Our noses are hooked up to hidden water tanks. You guys can't win!"

He tilted his head back. Water shot out of his nose and sprayed our table again.

"Ooh, we're scared. We're scared," I said, pretending to shake and quake. "You've got us shaking." I burst out laughing.

"Just wait. You won't be laughing when you're swimming for your lives!" The Big Sweety shouted.

What did he mean by that?

I took off my glasses, squeezed them—and shot water at Joe Sweety. I hit him in the front of his pants—in a very embarrassing place.

He looked down. Saw his wet pants. Shook a huge fist at me. And went running from the Dining Hall.

"Way to go, Big B!" Feenman and Crench both slapped me on the back.

22

But I didn't feel like celebrating. We were losing the war—big-time. How could we win against digital nose-squirters?

And I couldn't stop thinking about Joe Sweety's words ...

"You won't be laughing when you're swimming for your lives...."

What were those Nyce House dudes planning?

Chapter 5

MEET THE DEVASTATOR

It didn't take long to find out what Nyce House had planned.

After lunch I took a walk across the Great Lawn. Your school probably doesn't have a Great Lawn. It's a big green space with trees and a pond—like a small park in the middle of the campus.

I held my breath as I walked past smelly Pooper's Pond. (No one knows how it got that name.)

I turned and saw Sherman Oaks. He was scurrying across the grass with a large, gray tank bouncing on his back.

I jogged over to him. The thing on his back looked like a giant vacuum cleaner. He was groaning and moaning. It must have been heavy.

"Yo, Sherman!" I called. "What's up with the vacuum cleaner? Are you going to vacuum your money?"

He flashed me his shiny, sixty-five-toothed grin. I had to shield my eyes. Sherman is so rich, he has a guy come to his room to brighten his teeth once a week.

"You might as well surrender, Bernie," he said. "You and your Rotten House buddies have already lost the Water War." He snickered. "Hee-hee-hee."

I hate dudes who snicker—don't you?

"Sherman, have you been out in the sun too long?" I said. "Something has burned out your brain. There's *no way* you can win!"

"Hee-hee-hee." More snickering. "Bernie, see this thing on my back?"

"Very ugly," I said. "You should see a doctor and have it removed before it grows even bigger."

"I love it when you try to be funny," Sherman said, curling his lip in a sneer. "It's so cute. *Lame*, but cute."

"So what's up with the vacuum cleaner?" I asked.

"Actually, it's a twelve-gallon water tank," Sherman said. "It hooks up to this new Power Blaster my parents sent me."

He flashed me that blinding smile again. "My parents send me anything I ask for. They know I'm a spoiled brat. But they want me to be a *happy* spoiled brat!"

I tapped the water tank with a fist. It was full.

"I hook the tank up to the *Devastator*," Sherman said. He pulled out a red-and-blue water blaster. It looked like the nozzle at a gas station pump.

"The *Devastator* is more powerful than a fire hose. And it has a long-range viewfinder. So it can blast a kid up to a mile away." He pointed it at me and pretended to shoot it.

I gulped. "A mile?"

Sherman nodded. "Are you ready to surrender, Bernie? You'd better. If I blast you with the *Devastator*, it will change your whole bone structure. And you'll be about a foot shorter."

I tapped the water tank again. "You're not trying to scare me—*are* you, Sherman?"

He snickered. "Hee-hee-hee." It was an evil snicker.

I scratched my head. I pretended to be confused. "I don't get it," I said. "You hook up that thing to the tank, and it squirts? How does it work?"

"It's totally simple, dude," Sherman said. "Even *you* could work it. I'll show you."

He always likes to show off his new toys. Makes him feel like a big man. I scratched my head some more, pretending I didn't get it.

"Do you push this button here?" I asked.

"Not yet," Sherman said. "Here, Bernie. Try it on. I'll show you."

With a groan, he hoisted the heavy tank off his back. I helped him strap it onto my back. Then I watched him hook up the big, red-and-blue nozzle.

"Is this the shooter?" I asked. "Is this the part that blasts the water?"

It isn't easy for a genius like me to play dumb. But I can do it when I need to.

"Relax, dude," Sherman said. "It's simple. You just hold the nozzle and press this button."

I bit my lip. "I don't know. I don't think I can work it."

"Yes, you can," Sherman said. "Even a baby could

do it. You just push right here."

"Really?" I said. I aimed the nozzle at Sherman's chest.

"No! *Wait!*" Sherman cried.

I pushed the button.

WHHAAAAAAAAAAAMMMMMSSSSSHHHHHHH!

The blast of water was so powerful, it knocked me onto my back. Over the deafening roar, I could hear Sherman's screams of agony.

I sat up and took my finger off the button.

I blinked. Once. Twice.

Was I seeing what I was *seeing*?

Yes.

Sherman stood in front of me, dripping wet—
and totally naked!

*The water blast blew all his
clothes off!*

The only things he was
wearing were his *shoes!*

"Pretty good," I said. I handed him back his water blaster. "Not bad. It could use a little more power, though."

Sherman let out a weak gurgle.

I saw April-May June and a bunch of girls crossing the lawn. They stopped and pointed at Sherman. The girls uttered squeals of surprise. Then they started laughing their heads off.

Sherman gurgled again. He shook a fist at me. "You're toast, Bernie," he said. "Totally toast."

He glanced at the laughing girls. Then he ran off, trying to cover his butt as he ran.

The rumor is true! I saw. I clapped my hands to my face. Sherman really *did* have dollar signs tattooed on his butt!

As I watched the naked dude run, I knew he would try to get even with me.

Sure enough, he struck at lunch the next day....

Chapter 6

THE NAKED ASTRONAUT WINS

Sherman struck without warning.

My buddies Feenman, Crench, and I were having a quiet lunch in the Dining Hall. I was lapping up a big bowl of spaghetti. And I was showing my friends some really funny things you can do with meatballs.

I saw April-May June get up from her seat at the girls' table. She came walking toward me.

My tongue fell out of my mouth. I started to pant. April-May is my girlfriend. She's nuts about me. Only she doesn't know it yet. She doesn't have a clue.

I flashed her my best smile. "Yo, April-May," I said. "Whussup?"

She gave me a nice greeting. "No way, Bernie," she said.

"But I haven't *said* anything yet!" I replied.

"No way, Bernie," she said.

"Can I ask you a question?" I said.

She tossed back her blond hair. "No way, Bernie."

"I heard you all baked peanut-butter pies in

Cooking class," I said. I started to drool. I love peanut-butter pie. Some nights I dream about it.

"Wipe your chin, Bernie," April-May said. *The nicest thing she ever said to me.* She DOES care!

I wiped the drool off my chin with both hands.

"Do you think you could sneak out one of those pies for me?" I asked. "As a special favor?"

She sneered. "Bernie," she said, "I'd rather stick my fingers up my nose for a whole day."

"Does that mean you'll do it?" I asked.

April-May didn't have a chance to answer.

That's when Sherman burst into the Dining Hall. He raised a huge, new weapon. It looked like a giant slingshot. An enormous, blue balloon bounced on top of it.

"Stand back, everyone!" Sherman boomed. "It's gonna BLOW!"

"Hey, Sherman—looking good, dude! You're wearing your *pants* today!" Crench shouted.

Kids hooted with laughter.

You can't expect to stand totally naked on the Great Lawn and not get major laughs and hoots.

But the laughing stopped when Sherman raised the big slingshot.

"Stand back, everyone!" he shouted again. "This is no joke. It's rocket-powered!"

"Your *butt* is rocket-powered!" Feenman shouted. "Thanks for showing it to us yesterday!"

This time kids didn't laugh. A hush fell over the room. Everyone was staring at Sherman's rocket-powered slingshot.

"It's a water-balloon launcher," Sherman said. He struggled to hold it up in both hands. "My parents sent it to me because they want to buy my love. It cost two thousand dollars. It's rocket-powered. It uses NASA technology. And it can send a water balloon into *space*!"

A few kids gasped.

"Sherman, why don't you go up into space and try it out?" Feenman shouted. "You could be the first naked astronaut!"

"I'm gonna try it out right here!" Sherman shouted.

He raised the big slingshot. He pointed it at my table.

I heard a TWOINNNNG.

And then...

BA~BA~BA~
BOOOOOOOOOOOOM!

The giant blue water balloon shot across the room, spinning as it flew. It hit our table—and exploded!

"YAAAAIIIIIEEE!" I let out a horrified cry as a wave of water swept over us. My spaghetti bowl flew up into my face. Cold water gushed over me and splashed over the table.

When I finally pulled the spaghetti off my face, I saw Feenman and Crench frantically doing the breaststroke on the tabletop.

I spit out a mouthful of water and turned to the front of the room. My friends and I were soaked.

April-May stood a few feet away with Sherman and Wes Updood. They had their heads tossed back, and they were laughing...laughing their guts out.

I grabbed Feenman and Crench and dragged them to dry land. Then I raised both hands in surrender.

"Truce!" I shouted. "Truce!"

Crench grabbed me by my soaked school blazer. "Huh? Bernie? What's up with that? Are you really giving up?"

"You *never* give up!" Feenman cried. "Never!"

I brushed them both away. "Truce!" I shouted to Sherman. I kept my hands up high. "It's over. You win, Sherman. You win!"

Chapter 7

A SECRET WEAPON

I know. I know. This is supposed to be the story of how we got stuck with Mr. Skruloose, The Teacher from Heck. Well, I'm getting to it.

Just stick with me. I'm up to the good part of the story. I mean, the *bad* part. This is the part of the story where it all turned to *horror*.

We were in Rotten House. Everyone was gathered in my room on the third floor. That's because I'm the only kid in the dorm who has his own room.

I can't share. It makes me nervous. Besides, I need plenty of room to plot and scheme.

"Bernie, why did you call a truce? We can't quit," Feenman said. "We can't give up so easily."

"We can build our *own* rocket-powered water balloon launcher," Billy the Brain said. "You *know* I can build *anything*. Here, Big B—check this out. This can be our secret weapon."

He walked to the bed and woke up Gassy, my big bulldog. He tugged Gassy to his feet.

"Billy, that's my dog," I said. "How can he help us beat Nyce House?"

"Squeeze him," Billy said. He pushed me over to the dog. "Go ahead. Squeeze him."

"Are you NUTS?" Crench cried. "Don't squeeze him. The dog STINKS!"

"How do you think he got the name *Gassy?*" I said.

Billy tugged me over to the fat bulldog. "Go ahead. Squeeze his stomach."

"Okay, okay," I said. I reached down and wrapped my hands around my sweet dog's middle. I gave him a hard squeeze—*and water shot out of his butt!*

"I turned him into a squirt gun," Billy said. "The Nyce House dudes will never expect it! You'll take 'em totally by surprise."

41

I squeezed Gassy again. Another stream of water shot across the room.

"Dude, that's pretty clever," I said. "I like it. But ... you're too late."

The guys all stared at me. "Too late?" Belzer asked.

I nodded. "Sherman is on his way over here," I said. "He agreed to the truce. I told him Nyce House won."

"But, Bernie—" Feenman cried. "The war was just beginning. It's too early to surrender."

"Shh." I raised a finger to my lips. "I hear footsteps. Coming up the stairs."

We hurried out to the hall and listened for a few seconds.

"It's Sherman," I whispered, peering down the stairs.

"Bernie—don't give up the fight," Feenman whispered.

"We can beat them," Crench said.

"Sssshhhh!" I hushed them again. I could hear Sherman stop to take a breath on the second floor. Now he was starting up the stairs again.

Closer . . . one more step . . . then one more . . . I counted silently to myself. I waited until he made it to the eighth step. Then I reached up and grabbed the heavy rope I'd stretched along the ceiling.

I gave it a hard tug.

SPLOOOOOOSH!

I'd timed it perfectly. The giant water balloon perched over the eighth step crashed down on Sherman's head.

I heard a startled scream. The splash of cold water.

He hit the floor. I heard, "Gurgle, gurgle, gurgle."

"*YESSS!*"

I cried, jumping up and down. "Yesss! A direct hit! Bull's-eye!"

My buddies jumped to their feet, cheering, clapping, and laughing their heads off.

"Rotten House RULES!"

Belzer cried. "Bernie B. is still *king*!"

We all touched knuckles. Then we did the secret
Rotten House Handshake.

I heard the gurgling sound again. I turned and
gazed down the stairwell.

"Uh-oh—!"

I gasped in horror. Then I gasped again.

"Nooooo!" I wailed. "It can't be! It *can't* be!"

My buddies turned and stared. They saw what I
saw.

It wasn't Sherman on the stairs. It was *Mrs. Heinie*!

Mrs. Heinie on her knees, slipping and sliding on the wet stairs, soaked from head to foot. Mrs. Heinie, swept down the stairs by the water bomb. She stared up at us. Stared up at us and shook her fist.

"Uh-oh," Feenman muttered. "Think we're in trouble now?"

I let out a long, sad sigh. "Are we in trouble? Does a goose lay eggs in the woods?"

Chapter 8

"GOOD-BYE FOREVER!"

Mrs. Heinie roared up the stairs. She stood over us, dripping water. Her sopping wet hair drooped over her eyes. Water ran down her face. She shook both fists at us.

"You—you—you—" She made sputtering sounds.

Finally she brushed her hair back. Mopped her face with one hand. Straightened her drenched housedress.

Then she went berserk-o.

"I QUIT!" she screamed. "I—I can't TAKE it anymore!" She shook both fists in the air. She started pounding the wall with them.

"I QUIT! I QUIT! I QUIT!"

Bernie B. to the rescue. Other kids might try to hide when something like this happens. Not the Big B. I knew I could charm her.

I flashed her my best smile. "Mrs. H., your hair looks *lovely* when it's wet," I said. "The Damp Mop look really suits you. Awesome!"

"I quit! I quit! I QUIT!"

The old charm wasn't working yet. I took a deep breath and tried again. "I love those earrings. Are they new?"

"I'm not *wearing* earrings!" she screamed. "I have an infection on my earlobes!" She pounded her fists on the wall some more. "I quit! I'm *outta* here!"

"Mrs. H., let me explain what happened," I said. "We only did it because we LIKE you! It's just our way of saying what a good sport you are!"

"HAH!" she cried. Then with a wet swish, she turned and went screaming down the stairs. "I QUIT! I QUIT! GOOD-BYE FOREVER! I QUIT!"

Chapter 9

THE UPCHUCK GARDEN

That didn't go well. We knew we were in trouble.

A few minutes later, we heard Headmaster Upchuck's tiny shoes tapping on the stairs. And then he appeared in front of my door.

Everyone looks up to Headmaster Upchuck, even though he's only three feet tall. He's bald and has very pink skin and tiny black eyes. You could mistake him for a very big rodent, except that he wears a suit.

"What's going on here?" he demanded. "This is all *your* fault—isn't it, Bernie?"

I put on my best smile, stepped forward, and shook his little pink hand. "It's good to see you, sir," I said. "The guys and I were just saying how you never come visit us."

"Shut your piehole," he said.

"Very good, sir," I said, giving him a salute.

His pink face darkened to red. "I just want to know what happened to Mrs. Heinie."

Behind me, Feenman and Crench were trembling. They didn't want to be kicked out of school. I didn't like the idea, either.

"I can explain everything, sir," I said. "By the way, did you tie that bow tie yourself? That's brilliant, sir. It's upside down, but it's tied so beautifully!"

"Never mind my tie," Upchuck growled. "What happened here?"

"Poor Mrs. Heinie," I said, lowering my head. "It was a plumbing problem, you see. We don't like to cause the school janitors any trouble. So we were trying to fix the water pipe in the ceiling by ourselves. And poor Mrs. Heinie just happened to walk under the leaky pipe when—"

Headmaster Upchuck raised a hand to stop me.

"Bernie, let me say to you what I say to my darling, little grandchildren every day."

"What's that, sir?" I asked.

"Shut your yap."

"Yes, sir!" I said, saluting again.

"Bernie, I know it wasn't a plumbing problem," he said. "Sherman Oaks told me about your Water War."

I put on my most innocent, wide-eyed face. "Water War, sir? I don't know what you mean."

Upchuck turned to Belzer, who was shaking in a corner. "Belzer, *you* know about the Water War, don't you!" he said.

Belzer's chins quivered up and down. "*No hablo inglés!*" he cried. "*No hablo inglés!*"

Whenever Belzer gets scared, he pretends he doesn't speak English. It's kinda dumb, but sometimes it works.

Upchuck let out a growl. He turned back to me. "Sherman told me *you* started the whole thing, Bernie. What do you have to say about that?"

"It wasn't me, sir," I said. "I'm *allergic* to water. I have to stay dry at all times. Even when I take a shower."

Upchuck pointed at my school blazer. "Bernie, are you going to tell me that that flower on your lapel doesn't squirt water?"

"Of course not," I said. I fingered the yellow daisy on my blazer lapel. "I love flowers, sir. Everyone knows that about me. I'm planting a flower garden, and I'm naming it after you, sir. The Upchuck Garden."

Was he buying it? No.

He stared at the daisy on my jacket. "It's a squirting flower. I know it is," he muttered.

"No way," I insisted.

"*No hablo inglés!*" Belzer said again.

Headmaster Upchuck stepped forward. He reached out to squeeze my flower.

I was too fast for him. I backed away. But, whoa—! Look *out*! I tripped over Gassy. A gusher of water sprayed from the dog's butt—*and hit Upchuck right between the eyes!*

"Uh . . . I can explain that, sir," I said.

"NO, YOU CAN'T!" he screamed. He wiped water from his face. "Bernie, I know how to take care of you and your pals! You're doomed. DOOMED!"

"Surely you don't mean that, sir," I said. "We all know you have a *great* sense of humor. You can take a joke—right?"

"Ha-ha-ha," Upchuck said. "I'm going to be laughing, okay. I'm going to be laughing when you get your new teacher! Ha-ha-ha."

He turned and started down the stairs. And that's when the *second* water balloon fell from the ceiling.

SPLOOOOOOSH.

It plopped onto his head, flattened him to the stairs, and drenched him under a foot of cold water. The poor little guy was kicking and sputtering and swearing and swimming for his life.

I bent down to help him up. "I can explain, sir," I said.

But even the great Bernie B. couldn't talk his way out of this one.

And the next day, Headmaster Upchuck had his revenge. Mr. Skruloose, The Teacher from Heck, appeared....

Chapter 10

"You Students Are Lucky!"

So, Headmaster Upchuck sent Mrs. Heinie to the girls' dorm to be their dorm mother instead of ours. And he took her away from us fourth graders and made her a sixth-grade teacher.

And now Mr. Skruloose stood at the front of our class. He stood stiff as a broom with his big chest ballooning out of his school blazer. "Listen up, soldiers!" he bellowed, so loudly the windows rattled.

"I taught in the toughest military schools in the country," he said. "And I'm gonna whip you recruits into shape—if I have to *break* every one of you!"

Skruloose picked up a wooden yardstick and broke it over one knee.

"STOP STARING AT ME!" Skruloose screamed. "I don't like to be stared at, soldiers. Eyes straight ahead at all times."

I shut my eyes. *This is all a dream*, I thought. I'm gonna pinch myself, wake up, and Mrs. Heinie will be back.

I pinched myself. Then I opened my eyes.

Mr. Skruloose was scowling at me. "Did you just take a nap, soldier? I saw your eyes close."

"Uh...no, sir!" I cried.

This dude can't be serious, I told myself. He'll lighten up. I know he will.

Near the front of the room, I saw Billy the Brain take out his laptop. He set it on his desk and opened it.

Uh-oh, I thought. Did Billy forget something important about his laptop?

Billy pressed a key on the laptop. A stream of water shot out and sprayed April-May June in the face. She let out a startled scream and fell off her chair.

Yes, Billy *did* forget something. He forgot he turned his laptop into a squirt gun!

And now Mr. Skruloose stood over him, glaring down at the laptop.

"It's a keyboard problem," Billy said. "I have to call the help line after class."

Nice try, Brain.

"You need all the help you can get, soldier," Skruloose boomed. "Why don't you drop down to the floor. Let's see how many push-ups you can do in an hour."

"An hour?" Billy gasped. "But that's sixty minutes!"

I *told* you he was a brain.

With a sigh, Billy started to lower himself to the floor. But he bumped the laptop—and it squirted April-May again.

She let out another scream.

Billy settled onto his stomach and tried to do a push-up. I knew he could do maybe one or two in an hour. The dude is a brain, remember—not a jock.

Mr. Skruloose returned to his desk. "I heard about your Water War," he snarled, "and it's all over. Let me repeat that. OVER!"

He picked up the broken yardstick and cracked it into tiny pieces.

That sent a shiver down my back. He really liked *breaking* things.

This isn't fair, I thought. How can Skruloose end the Water War? It's *our* turn to attack. We haven't had a chance to get back at Sherman for flooding out our lunch. He can't let Sherman and Nyce House win!

"You soldiers will survive my class—if you follow my simple rules," Mr. Skruloose boomed.

From his front-row seat, Sherman Oaks waved another hundred-dollar bill in Skruloose's face. "Maybe this little gift will convince you to skip me," Sherman said. "I'm way too rich to follow any rules."

Skruloose totally ignored Sherman. Once again he began listing his classroom rules:

"Both feet on the floor at all times, shoes at a forty-five-degree angle. Posture counts for twenty-five percent of your grade. No unnecessary smiling. No licking your lips."

Nice.

"I will be giving you *four hours* of homework every night, seven nights a week," Mr. Skruloose announced. "You students are lucky. I *used* to be *strict!*"

Chapter 11

GASSY HAS TO GO

After dinner Feenman and Crench slumped into my room. They dropped onto my bed, sighing and shaking their heads.

"Sherman is bragging to everyone that he won the Water War," Feenman said. "He's telling everyone you surrendered."

I groaned. "What can I do? Mr. Skruloose said the Water War was over. Do you want me to go argue with him? You saw what he did to that yardstick."

"We don't have time for a Water War, anyway,"

Crench said. "We have so much homework."

"Four hours of homework every night?" Feenman moaned. "I can't do it, Bernie. All that reading hurts my eyes."

"I can't think that long," Crench said. "If I try to think for more than a few minutes, I get a headache." He pounded his forehead.

A shadow fell over the room. Mr. Skruloose burst in, breathing hard, pointing at my two buddies. "No slouching on the beds!" he barked. "Sit up. Posture! Posture!"

Feenman and Crench pulled themselves up straight.

Skruloose lowered his eyes to their bare feet. "Where are your shoes?" he boomed. "I don't like to see feet in my dorm."

"Mrs. Heinie always let us go b-barefoot," Crench stammered.

Mr. Skruloose made a disgusted face. "Mrs. Heinie? Who is Mrs. Heinie? *I'm* in charge now. And I'll *kick* your heinie if I see any bare feet in here again."

"Y-yes, sir," Crench muttered.

I tried to change the subject. "Sir, we're just so totally *pumped* to have you here," I said. "We know you're going to do *great things* here at Rotten House."

He frowned at me. "Great things? With a bunch of *losers* like you?" He shook a big, meaty fist in the air. "But don't worry," he said. "I'll shape you soldiers up. When I'm finished, you won't recognize yourselves."

All three of us made gulping sounds.

"Stand at attention!" he boomed. "I'm going to do the inspection now!"

He brushed the three of us out of his way. "I heard about your Water War," he said. "I'm searching your rooms every night. If I find any squirt guns or water blasters, you will report to Headmaster Upchuck to be sent home."

All three of us made gulping sounds again.

Skruloose pulled out a flashlight, dropped to the floor, and searched under my bed. "What's *this?*" he cried.

Uh-oh. Gassy. My big, fat bulldog.

Think fast, Bernie. Think fast.

There are no pets allowed in the Rotten School dorms.

"Uh…I confess, sir," I said. "It's a water balloon."

Skruloose kept the flashlight trained on Gassy. "A water balloon?" he boomed. "But…it has a face. And it's staring back at me. And … PHEW … it *stinks*!"

"No, sir," I said. "It's a water balloon. Trust me."

I reached down and dragged Gassy out to the middle of the floor. "It looks a lot like a dog," I said, "but it's not. Go ahead. Squeeze it, sir. You'll see. It squirts water."

"It's a dog," Skruloose insisted. "A fat, smelly dog."

"Squeeze it," I said. "You'll see."

Mr. Skruloose bent down. He wrapped his hands around Gassy's fat belly—and squeezed.

BRRRRAAAAA AAAAAAPPPPH!

"Ooh, it stinks! It STINKS!" Feenman and Crench wailed, holding their noses.

I guess Billy the Brain forgot to fill up Gassy's water tank.

"No dogs in the dorm, soldier," Mr. Skruloose said. He pointed to the door. "Take it outside. The dog has to sleep outside."

I gasped. "Outside? He can't, sir," I said. "The fresh air gives him a cough."

"Outside," Mr. Skruloose insisted.

Gassy gazed up at me with those sad, brown eyes. I didn't want to part with my sweet pet. But I had no choice. I shouted out the door. "Belzer! Belzer, get in here! Take Gassy outside."

Belzer hurried in. He threw the fat bulldog over his shoulder and disappeared with him. I could hear Gassy whimpering all the way down the stairs.

Or was that Belzer?

"No more Mr. Nice Guy!" Mr. Skruloose screamed. "I'm going to get tough now!"

Uh-oh.

"Now get your shoes, soldiers!" Skruloose yelled. "We'll have a lesson. You need to polish your shoes for an hour every night. We want those shoes to shine in a dark closet—don't we?"

"Yes, sir," we said.

We polished our shoes for an hour. Then Mr. Skruloose made us put them in a dark closet to make sure they glowed. Finally he headed down to the second floor to shape up the dudes down there.

Feenman, Crench, and I slumped to the floor. Sweat poured down our faces. Our trembling hands were black from shoe polish.

Crench sighed. "He's gotta go," he murmured. "We can't survive this."

I sighed, too. "He sent away my poor doggy. At least he didn't see my parrot." I pointed to Lippy in his cage on my dresser. "Lippy would never survive outside. He's too delicate."

"GO SUCK A CUTTLEBONE!" the adorable prettyboy cried. "SUCK A CUTTLEBONE—AND CHOKE!"

He's so cute.

Feenman tore at his long, scraggly hair. "Now there's *no way* we can win the Water War. Not with Skruloose looking under our beds every night."

Through the open window I could hear Gassy, my poor pet. Out in the cold, dark night all by himself. Whimpering softly. Coughing.

"We've gotta get rid of Skruloose—fast," I said.

Feenman grabbed the front of my shirt. "Bernie, do you have a plan?"

I flashed him a grin. "Does a monkey have chapped lips? Of *course* I have a plan!"

Chapter 12

WHY I SOBBED AND BAWLED

The next day I started to put my plan into effect.

I found April-May June in the kitchen of the Home Arts room. She was stacking peanut-butter pies on a shelf. I counted at least a dozen of them.

Perfect. I needed only one.

April-May's mouth dropped open when she saw me, and she gave me a warm greeting. "Beat it, Bernie."

She loves to tease me. That's how I know she likes me.

"You're looking hot," I said.

"You're looking *not*," she replied.

Ha-ha. I love a girl with a sense of humor.

She straightened her blazer over her pleated school skirt.

"The Rotten School colors look awesome on you," I said. "They match your eyes."

She stared at me. "Huh? Green, yellow, and purple?"

I saw Ms. Sally Monella, the Cooking teacher, watching us from across the room. "I need one of those peanut-butter pies," I whispered to April-May.

"And I need a second nose," April-May replied. She turned away from me and started stacking pies again.

"No. Really," I said. "It's not for me, April-May. I swear."

"You're right, Bernie," she said. "They're not for you."

"Just one!" I pleaded.

Ms. Monella walked over to us. "Bernie, how y'all doing?" she asked. She's tall and young and pretty, and she's from the South.

"I'm doing fine," I said, my eyes on the peanut-butter pies. Then I remembered something about

Ms. Monella. She's a sucker for any kid who cries.

She's totally tenderhearted. She can't say no to anyone who bawls and sobs.

"Well, what y'all doin' here?" Ms. Monella asked.

"I—I—I—" I pretended to stutter. Then I burst into tears and sobbed and bawled as loudly as I could. I covered my face with both hands and let my whole body shake.

"WWWHAAAAAAAAAAAAAAAH!"

"Bernie? Bernie? What's wrong?" Ms. Monella cried.

I wiped the tears from my eyes. "Those p-peanut-butter pies," I said in a shaky voice. "They smell just like the pies my mother used to bake…."

"They do?" Ms. Monella said. "How nice to have such sweet memories."

I let a few more tears run down my cheeks.

April-May was watching me carefully. "He's faking," she told Ms. Monella.

But Ms. Monella didn't hear her. She reached up and pulled a peanut-butter pie down from the shelf. "Here ya go, Bernie," she said softly. "Y'all enjoy this, ya hear?"

"Thank you, thank you," I said in a trembling whisper. I grabbed the pie and ran out of the room.

Time for Part Two of my brilliant plan.

I met Feenman, Crench, and Belzer in my dorm room. "Success!" I cried. "I got the pie."

Feenman had a fork in each hand. That's one of his big talents. He eats with both hands at once. "Let's DIG IN!" he shouted.

"Back! Back!" I had to shove them all back. "It's not for you."

All three of them groaned. "You got a peanut-butter pie? And you're not gonna share it?"

"I'm not going to *eat* it, either," I said. "Back! Get BACK!" I gave Feenman a hard push. He was drooling on the pie.

"Who's it for?" Crench asked.

"Mr. Skruloose," I said.

Crench blinked. "Huh? You're giving *him* a pie?"

"That's my brilliant plan," I said. "We're going to make him feel welcome, dudes. We're gonna *charm* him."

Feenman rolled his eyes. "Whoa. That's supposed to be brilliant?" he muttered.

"Listen," I said. "No one can resist the Bernie Bridges charm. You know that. Once he gets a taste of the old charm, he'll soften up. He'll turn into a good guy. A pussycat!"

All three of them squinted at me.

"Have faith, dudes!" I said. "Have FAITH. Have I ever let you down before?"

"Never!" Belzer shouted. "Never!"

"Right! Now let's go find Skruloose," I said. "This is going to be awesome." I held the pie in front of me and led the way down the stairs.

Chapter 13

PEANUT–BUTTER PIE

We found Mr. Skruloose downstairs in the Commons Room. That's our living room, with a couch and big armchairs, game tables, a fridge with snacks, and a big TV. A place to hang out when we're not doing our *four hours* of homework.

Skruloose was talking to some second graders. He was telling them his rules for how to relax. "Take deep breaths. Keep your legs marching in a fast tempo. Chest out. Back straight..."

The second graders looked tense. They ran away as soon as my buddies and I entered the room.

Mr. Skruloose turned to us. "Finished your homework already, soldiers? Maybe I should start giving more!"

Time to turn on the charm. I held the pie up to Mr. Skruloose. "We baked this for you with our own hands, sir," I said. "It's our Welcome to Rotten House gift. Just our way of showing how much we care."

Skruloose blinked a couple of times. He stared at the pie. His neck muscles rippled. "That's very nice of you soldiers," he said.

"See? It's working!" I whispered to my buddies. "I *told* you!"

Mr. Skruloose took one of Feenman's forks. He dipped it into the pie, pulled out a big hunk, and shoved it into his mouth.

"Enjoy it, sir," I said. "We worked hard on it because we all like you so much."

Skruloose took another forkful, then another. He made loud chewing noises and gulped when he swallowed.

"Not bad, soldiers," he said. "Mmm. Not bad. What kind of pie is this?"

"It's peanut-butter pie, sir," I said. "We crushed the peanuts ourselves. Nothing is too good for you, sir!"

Mr. Skruloose let out a hoarse cry. Then he spit a glob of pie across the room.

"Is anything the matter, sir?" I asked.

"ARE YOU TRYING TO *KILL* ME? I'M ALLERGIC TO PEANUTS!" he screamed. "If I eat only *one tiny peanut*, my head swells up like a balloon, my skin peels off, and my eyes start twirling in my head."

He stuck a finger down his throat and made gross gagging sounds.

"Perhaps we made a bad choice, sir," I said. "But it's the *thought* that counts—right? Our hearts were in the right place."

"AAAAAAGGGGGH!"

He let out an angry scream. I don't think my charm was working.

"All three of you—" he shouted. "Thirty laps around the house while I run to the nurse and have my stomach pumped!"

He ran out the front door screaming.

I turned to my buddies. "Okay, okay," I said. "Plan B."

Chapter 14

PLAN B

But I didn't have a Plan B.

I thought about it all day. We couldn't charm Skruloose. We *had* to get rid of him. But *how*?

I was still thinking about it after dinner in my room while Belzer massaged my toes. See, sometimes when I think *too* hard, I get toe cramps. Luckily, Belzer is around to do his magic-fingers trick and loosen up my toe muscles.

Good kid, Belzer.

He was down on the floor, concentrating on my little piggies. "Belzer, what's that T-shirt you're wearing?" I asked. "Let me see it."

He raised himself so I could read the front of the shirt: PLEASE SLAP MY FACE.

"Belzer, that's a loser shirt," I said.

He blinked. "You think so?"

"It's totally gross," I said. "Where did you get it?"

"It was a birthday present," he replied. "From my grandma."

"Cover it up," I said. "I'm trying to think. There's *gotta* be a way to get rid of Skruloose."

Belzer went to work on the little baby toes. "Gentle! Gentle!" I said. "They're attached to my feet, you know!"

"I have an idea," Belzer said. "Mrs. Heinie quit because she got flattened by a water balloon—right?"

"Right," I said.

"So why don't we drop one on Skruloose?" Belzer said. "Then he'll quit, too."

I patted him on the head. "Belzer, I warned you, remember? Your brain is not quite ripe enough for thinking. Maybe in a year or two. Until then you should rest it, okay?"

"Okay, Bernie," he said. "How do the toes feel?"

I wiggled them. "Like new," I said. "Thank you! You can put on my shoes and socks now."

The toes felt so good, I went for a walk around the campus. Sometimes walking helps me think.

It was a clear, warm night. As I crossed the little bridge over the water, the moonlight reflected like silver in Pooper's Pond.

And in the light, I recognized two figures on the other side of the pond. They were walking near R.U. Dumm Field, our football field.

Mr. Skruloose. And my half-human friend Beast.

Why were *they* hanging out together? I slid behind a tree where I could watch them.

Beast was crouched down on all fours. Not unusual. Sometimes he walks like that for days.

Mr. Skruloose had a hand on Beast's shoulder. Suddenly, he shouted, "Go get him, soldier! GO!"

Beast let out a low growl. Then he took off, running on all fours—chasing a squirrel!

"Go! Go, soldier! Go!" Mr. Skruloose cheered him on.

Beast growled and grunted as he rumbled over the grass. The poor squirrel didn't stand a chance.

"YES!" Mr. Skruloose pumped his fists in the air when Beast caught the squirrel in his teeth. "Yes! Yes! VICTORY!"

Beast let the squirrel go. He never knew what to do with them after he caught them. He turned to Skruloose with a big grin on his face. He still had some fur caught in his teeth.

Skruloose patted him on the back.

He LIKES Beast! I realized.

That started the Bernie B. brain buzzing. I was thinking hard—so hard, I started to sweat. In a flash I had Plan B.

Why does Mr. Skruloose like Beast? Because he's fierce. Ferocious. Because he's gung ho, a *good soldier*.

What if we *all* act gung ho? What if we *all* act like soldiers?

Then Mr. Skruloose will *like* us. And he'll stop being so strict. He'll lighten up and stop being The Teacher from Heck.

Sure, it was a crazy idea. But it was definitely worth a try....

Chapter 15

YUMMY TREE BARK

I started Plan B the next night. I gathered all the guys in the Study Hall downstairs. The chairs were covered in cobwebs. Most of us had never *seen* the Study Hall.

"What are we doing here, Bernie?" Feenman asked.

"Wait. Just wait," I said, watching the door. I waited until Mr. Skruloose was nearby.

"Okay, soldiers, listen up!" I shouted. "We're doing our math homework. Crench—multiplication tables. Go!"

"Uh...okay," Crench muttered. "I—"

"You forgot to salute," I said. "Next time you forget . . . thirty push-ups!"

Crench saluted.

"Go. Start multiplying, soldier!" I barked.

"Well . . . uh . . . four times four is eleven. Four times five is twelve. Four—"

"Did you forget something, soldier?" I cried. "Did you forget to say *sir*?"

"Sorry, sir," Crench said. He saluted again.

I peered into the hall and saw that Mr. Skruloose had a big smile on his face. He was totally *into* it! He liked it!

"Feenman, go! Multiply!" I ordered.

"Yes, sir!" Feenman gave me a long salute. "Four times six is twenty. Four times seven—"

"It's okay. You can stop," I said. "Skruloose is gone."

We all breathed long sighs of relief.

"Bernie, this is crazy," Feenman said. "We're not soldiers. We're kids. We can't act like soldiers all the time."

"Yes, we can—when Skruloose is watching," I said. "You should have seen the smile on his face. He was *eating it up!*"

"But it hurts my head to salute so much," Feenman said.

Thunk!

"Try doing it more softly," I told him. "And don't use your fist next time. Just use two fingers."

"I'll try that," Feenman said, rubbing his forehead.

I saw Mr. Skruloose return. "Okay, soldiers!" I shouted. "Attention! Stand at attention. We meet at the front door tomorrow morning at 0800 hours, and we—"

"What does that mean? 0800?" Belzer asked. "I can't find that on my watch, Bernie."

"Eight o'clock, soldier!" I said. "We'll march to class. I want everyone in a perfect single file. That will be all!"

Everyone saluted. Feenman punched himself in the head again. He just couldn't get it.

Mr. Skruloose flashed me a thumbs-up as I headed to the front stairs.

Bernie, you're a genius! I told myself. If only my arm was long enough to pat myself on the back!

The next morning I gathered all the Rotten House dudes in a straight line at 0800 hours, and I marched them across the Great Lawn to class.

"Left, right! Left, right!" I called out. "Feenman, stand up straight! Chipmunk, stop staring at the ground."

"But, Bernie," Chipmunk whined, "the sun's in my eyes!"

I saw Skruloose hurrying toward us. "Move, soldiers!" I commanded. "Left, right! Left, right! Double speed! March!"

"Halt!" I cried. They stopped, tripping and stumbling over one another.

I turned to Mr. Skruloose. "Just trying to shape them up, sir," I said. "We want you to be proud of us."

Skruloose rubbed his chin. "Hmm. You've given me a great idea, soldier," he said.

I saluted him again. "*All* of your ideas are great, sir," I said. "That's why we guys want to be just like you."

Mr. Skruloose nodded. "Well, since you like the military way so much," he said, "you and your guys can form a drill team."

My mouth dropped open. "Excuse me? A *what*?"

"A drill team," Skruloose said. "You'll learn to

march together. Right face. Left face. Forward. Back. You'll love it."

He slapped me on the back. "Everyone up before the sun every morning. Onto the practice field. Two hours of drills every morning before breakfast."

I choked. "Before breakfast? But, sir, I have breakfast in bed every morning. It's the most important meal of the day, you know."

Mr. Skruloose didn't hear me. He slapped me on the back again. "Yes. A drill team. Two hours of marching across the field every morning. Thanks for the great idea, Bridges."

"Please don't thank me, sir," I muttered.

"And you've given me another idea," he said.

Uh-oh.

"I'm putting your whole dorm on a special tree-bark diet," Skruloose said. "Tree bark three times a day. To toughen you up!"

He marched away.

I turned to my friends. "I know, I know," I said. "Plan C."

Chapter 16

"PASS THE TREE BARK?"

A few nights later I lay in bed, thinking...thinking. I was desperate now. I knew none of us could survive much longer.

Through my open window, I could hear my poor dog, Gassy, out in the cold. Coughing his head off from all that fresh air.

And what was that other alarming sound? It was my stomach growling, from eating only tree bark. Tree bark three times a day. *Raw*—not even cooked!

My stomach rumbled and grumbled. Every muscle in my body ached from two hours of drill practice every morning. My head ached, too, from four hours of homework.

And there was no time to get our revenge on Sherman Oaks. He was still bragging to everyone that he'd won the Water War.

This had to stop. Skruloose had to go.

Okay, dudes. Plan C.

Headmaster Upchuck has a tiny, red brick house next to the School House. He and his wife live upstairs. His office is downstairs.

The next morning I made my way to Upchuck's house. Could I talk him into getting rid of Skruloose? I had to try.

"My door is always open."

That's what Headmaster Upchuck always says. "If you have a problem, come see me. My door is always open."

So I walked up to the white front door. Sure enough, a sign above the door read: MY DOOR IS ALWAYS OPEN.

I tried the doorknob and pushed. Then I pulled.

The door was locked.

I read the sign again. I knocked on the door, softly

at first, then with pounding fists.

"Who's there?" Headmaster Upchuck called.

I saw an eye peek out of the little, round peephole. Then I heard him groan. "Oh, no. Please tell me it isn't *you* again!"

"Yes, it's me. Good morning, sir," I said brightly. "May I come in?"

A long silence. Then he said, "Would you believe there's no one here?"

"No," I said. "I see your eye peeping out at me. And I can hear you."

"Oh. Okay. Well…can you slip it under the door, Bernie?"

"No, sir. I need to talk to you, sir," I said. "If you could open the door …?"

"I put a lot of locks on the door, Bernie," he said. "You know. To keep you out in case you ever came back here."

"Well, I'm back, sir," I said. "I'd love to see your handsome face again. It always inspires me, sir. And I need to talk to you about something important."

"I was afraid of that," Headmaster Upchuck said.

"What if I *begged* you to go away, Bernie? Would that work?"

"No, sir," I said.

The Headmaster's eye disappeared from the peephole. Then I heard *click-click-click*. The sound of twenty locks being unlocked.

The door swung open. I gazed down at the little guy.

"Thank you, sir," I said. "You're looking good today. Is that a new sweater? I like it! They have some great new styles in the little boys' department—don't they? I won't take up your time, sir. I just have a quick question."

The Headmaster sighed. "The last time you had a 'quick question', it cost me a fortune. I had to build a hot tub for the boys in your dorm."

"They were desperate, sir," I replied. "They couldn't relax without it, sir. It saved their lives. We're so grateful. We named it after you, sir. The Upchuck Tub."

Upchuck shook his head. He was speechless.

"May I come in, sir?" I asked.

"No, Bernie. Stand back," he said. "You can't see

it, but I put an electric fence across the doorway. To keep you out. Take two steps forward, and you'll be *fried*."

"I see, sir. Very clever," I said. "Well, perhaps I could talk to you right here. You see, it's about Mr. Skruloose, sir."

The Headmaster clenched his teeth. "What about him?"

"He's treating us like soldiers, sir," I said. "He's cruel. He's heartless. He's a maniac."

Headmaster Upchuck smiled. "He *is*?"

"Yes, sir. He makes us march for two hours every morning. He makes us run laps around the dorm. He makes us do push-ups in class. He feeds us nothing but tree bark!"

Upchuck burst out laughing. "That's *wonderful*!" he cried. He jumped up and down happily. "Wonderful news. The man knows how to do his job! He's a genius! Thanks for brightening my day, Bernie!"

"Yes, sir!" I said, and I gave the Headmaster a salute. "We love it, sir. It's just what we need!"

"Huh?" Upchuck's smile vanished. His whole body sank.

"We need the discipline, sir," I said. "We need the hard work. We *love* having a teacher who whips us into shape!"

Upchuck's tiny eyes bulged. "You...you DO? You *love* it?"

"Please don't ever take him away from us, sir," I said. "We need him, sir. The guys all love him. If you brought Mrs. Heinie back, it would be a punishment. A terrible punishment."

Upchuck rubbed his chin. I could see he was thinking hard. "It would be a punishment?" he asked. "Really?"

"Really," I said. "A terrible punishment."

"Thanks for telling me, Bernie." He closed the door in my face. I could hear him chuckling through the door. I recognized that evil chuckle.

"Yes!" I whispered, pumping my fists into the air. "Yesss! Bernie B., you're still a genius!"

I hurried back to Rotten House. Feenman and Crench were finishing breakfast.

"Want some tree bark, Bernie?" Crench asked. "I saved you some soft pieces."

"Forget the tree bark," I said. "We'll all be eating

peanut-butter pie again real soon." I grinned my famous grin at them. "Check your watches, dudes. Trust your leader. Life will be sweet again by tomorrow morning!"

SAD NEWS

"Left, right! Left, right, Left! Eyes front!"

Mr. Skruloose barked out the rhythm as he marched us across the field. "Stand up straight, soldiers! We had to march in total darkness. The sun wasn't up yet. My stomach growled. My legs ached. But I was happy. I had a smile on my face.

I kept checking my watch. I knew what would happen next.

And, yes, here he came. Headmaster Upchuck, trotting across the grass, his gray suit jacket flapping behind him.

"Soldiers, halt!" Mr. Skruloose shouted as the Headmaster ran up to us. We all stopped, breathing hard, drenched in sweat.

Upchuck saluted Mr. Skruloose. Then he turned to us. "Boys, I have sad news," Upchuck said.

I stepped forward. "Sir, may we keep marching?" I said. "We love to march. Marching for two hours is the best part of our day."

Skruloose picked me up and dropped me back with the other guys. "Be quiet, Bridges," he said. "Let the Headmaster get a word in."

"Of course, sir," I said, saluting. "See, Headmaster Upchuck? See how we love it when Mr. Skruloose gives us orders? Do you think maybe we could march for *three* hours today?"

Upchuck cleared his throat and pulled himself up to his full three-foot height. "Sorry, boys. Bad news. Mr. Skruloose is too good to be wasted on you

Rotten House bums."

"Yes, he's brilliant, sir," I said. "That's why we need him. That's why we'd follow him anywhere." I saluted again.

Upchuck turned to me. "Thank you, Bernie, for telling me how brilliant Mr. Skruloose is. Because of that, I'm taking him *away* from Rotten House—and from the fourth grade. And I'm naming him *Assistant Headmaster!*"

Whoa. I hadn't planned on that. But, okay. As long as Skruloose was out of Rotten House . . .

I had to make sure. I dropped to my knees and started to beg. "Please, sir, don't take him away from us. We don't want him to leave."

Upchuck chuckled. "If *you* want him, Bernie, I have no choice. Say good-bye to him."

"Good-bye!" we all shouted at once.

Mr. Skruloose gave us a long salute. "Keep eating that tree bark, soldiers," he said. "You look tougher already. I'll miss you guys."

He started walking away with Headmaster Upchuck.

"We won't forget you, sir," I called. "Can we help

you pack your bags? We know you'll want to hurry—won't you, sir?"

We didn't start celebrating—laughing and cheering and high-fiving and slapping knuckles and hooting and rolling around on the grass—until the two of them were out of sight.

Chapter 18

WHO WINS THE WATER WAR?

The next morning I awoke with a smile. Sunlight poured through my window. Belzer came in humming, carrying my breakfast tray.

"I didn't know if you wanted eggs or French toast," he said.

"Just put the eggs on *top* of the French toast," I said. "Pour the syrup on gently...gently. Just a drizzle. Did you take the pulp out of my orange juice?"

"Of course," he said. "I strained it twice, and I drank half of it—just to make sure." He set the tray on my lap.

"A beautiful day!" I said. "No marching. No tree bark."

I hugged Gassy. He was tucked under the covers next to me. I slipped him a slice of bacon. He burped in my face—his cute way of saying thanks.

Feenman and Crench came bursting in. Feenman made a grab for my French toast. I had to stab him with my fork to keep him away.

"How great is this?" Crench cried. "No more tree bark. Skruloose is gone, and everything is back to normal!"

I handed the tray to Belzer and climbed out of bed. "One more thing to do," I said. "Finish the Water War."

"Huh? Finish it?" Crench said.

"I invited Sherman over here," I said. "To congratulate him on his victory."

They stared at me. "Bernie, have you totally lost it?" Feenman asked.

"Sherman's victory will last until he reaches the eighth step," I said. "I rigged up the water balloon in the ceiling again. When he reaches the eighth step, I pull the rope. Sploosh. Sherman sinks under ten gallons of cold water. We win—big-time."

"Brilliant!" Belzer said. "Then everything *will* be back to normal!"

I heard footsteps from downstairs. "He's here!" I whispered. "Feenman—quick. Get your camera. I want to e-mail this photo to everyone in school!"

Feenman disappeared into his room. The rest of us hurried out into the hall. I leaned over the banister and gazed down the stairs. "Shh. Quiet, dudes. Here he comes."

Feenman raised his camera.

"Wait for it. Wait for it...." I whispered.

I grabbed the rope. I counted and listened to Sherman's heavy shoes clomp up the stairs.

"Wait for it...wait...NOW!"

I tugged the rope hard. The camera flashed.

SPAAAALOOO OOOOOOSH!

I heard a startled scream. The splash of cold water.

He hit the floor. He made a choked sound.

"YESSS!" I cried, jumping up and down. "Yesss! A direct hit! Bull's-eye!"

My buddies jumped to their feet, cheering, clapping, and laughing their heads off.

We all touched knuckles. Then we did the secret Rotten House Handshake.

I heard the gurgling sound again.

GURGLE
GURGLE

I turned and gazed down the stairwell.

"Uh-oh—!" I gasped in horror. Then I gasped again.

"Mrs. Heinie?" I called. "Mrs. Heinie? You're back? Welcome back, Mrs. Heinie. What a surprise. I can explain! Really! I can explain!"

HERE'S A SNEAK PEEK AT BOOK #9 IN

R.L. STINE'S

ROTTEN SCHOOL

Duck Plop

"OOF!"

I landed on my stomach. My breath shot out in a painful *whoosh!* With a groan, I spun around and glanced behind me.

I saw my friend Feenman running across the grass. He was hugging a big, brown duck in his arms. The duck was quacking its head off and snapping at Feenman's ears.

"Duck, Bernie!" he shouted.

I pushed myself to my feet. I brushed dirt off the knees of my khakis. "Feenman," I said, "where did you get that duck?"

"I found it," he said.

The duck quacked and chewed off a big hunk of Feenman's brown hair.

"You'd better set it free," I said. "It doesn't like you."

Feenman's mouth dropped open. "Set it free? But I *found* it! It's mine!"

Feenman is not the brightest candle on the cake. If we are talking brains, the duck would win.

Feenman squeezed the duck a little too hard. It dropped a disgusting mess onto his shoes.

"Bernie, are you going to the hard-boiled egg-eating contest Friday?" Feenman asked. "Are you gonna bet on Beast?"

Our friend Beast can eat anything. Last year he ate *forty-two* hard-boiled eggs before he barfed his guts out.

I made a *ton* of money betting on the dude.

"I don't have time for the contest," I said. "I've got to find April-May. I want to go with her to the All-Nighter."

"It's a girl-ask-boy party," Feenman said. "If a girl

doesn't ask you, you can't go!"

"April-May is *desperate* to ask me," I said. "She just doesn't know it yet."

The duck snapped off another hunk of Feenman's hair. "Did you hear what they're planning?" he asked. "A huge barbeque. A soccer game on R.U. Dumm Field—boys against girls. Then a three-legged race across Pooper's Pond. And a treasure hunt in the dark for BIG prizes."

I rubbed my hands together. "I gotta get to that party," I said. "I have a special reason. I'll show you why."

I saw my buddy Belzer staggering under the two huge cartons he was carrying for me. You don't expect Bernie B. to carry two fifty-pound cartons, do you?

"Belzer—come over here!" I shouted.

He stumbled forward. "Hunh-hunh-hunh." He was gasping for breath. "Hunh-hunh." Sweat poured off his pudgy face.

"Okay. You can set 'em down for a minute," I said.

Belzer lowered the cartons. Then he fell facedown onto the grass in a dead faint.

"Feenman, put down the duck," I said. "Check this out."

He hugged the duck tighter. "Maybe we can cook it," he said.

"Feenman, we're kids—remember? Kids don't cook duck."

He nodded. "Yeah. You're right. I don't wanna eat duck, anyway. All those feathers would get stuck in my teeth."

"Drop it," I said. "Before *it* drops another pile of plop on your shoes."

Oops. Too late.

Feenman finally opened his arms and set the duck free. It tore across the grass, flapping and squawking.

"Feenman, come over here," I said. I tugged open one of the cartons. "This is why I've gotta get to the All-Nighter. Check this out...."

ABOUT THE AUTHOR

photo by Dan Nelken

R.L. Stine graduated from the Rotten School with a solid D+ average, which put him at the top of his class. He says that his favorite activities at school were Scratching Body Parts and Making Armpit Noises.

In sixth grade, R.L. won the school Athletic Award for his performance in the Wedgie Championships. Unfortunately, after the tournament, his underpants had to be surgically removed.

R.L. was very popular in school. He could tell this because kids always clapped and cheered whenever he left the room. One of his teachers remembers him fondly: "R.L. was a hard worker. He was so proud of himself when he learned to wave bye-bye with both hands."

After graduation, R.L. became well known for writing scary book series such as The Nightmare Room, Fear Street, Goosebumps, and Mostly Ghostly, and a short story collection called *Beware!*

Today, R.L. lives in a cage in New York City, where he is busy writing stories about his school days. Says he: "I wish everyone could be a Rotten Student."

for more information
about R.L. Stine,
go to www.rottenschool.com
and www.rlstine.com

ENTER THE
BE-A-ROTTEN-CHARACTER
CONTEST
AT ROTTENSCHOOL.COM

SOMEONE NEW IS COMING
TO ROTTEN SCHOOL . . .

and it could be you! Enter today for a chance to be a character in a future ROTTEN SCHOOL book, and join Bernie Bridges, Sherman Oaks, April-May June, and the rest of the kids at the rottenest school around!

Log on to **www.rottenschool.com** to enter. The winner's name will appear in a future ROTTEN SCHOOL book, and the winner will receive a set of ROTTEN SCHOOL books signed by R.L. Stine.

R.L. STINE WILL PICK
THE WINNER!

No purchase necessary. Entries must be received between August 22 and November 1, 2006.

One grand-prize winner will receive signed copies of all the books in the series and see his or her name in *Rotten School #12*. Three runners-up will win all the books in the series signed by R.L. Stine.

For the Official Rules and other details, visit **www.rottenschool.com**.